TITLES AVAILABLE IN BUZZ BOOKS

First published 1990 by Buzz Books,
an imprint of the Octopus Publishing Group,
Michelin House, 81 Fulham Road, London SW3 6RB

LONDON   MELBOURNE   AUCKLAND

Looney Tunes, the Looney Tunes character names, likenesses and
slogans are trademarks of Warner Bros Inc. © 1990 Warner Bros Inc.
This edition copyright © William Heinemann Ltd 1990
Reprinted 1991

ISBN 1 85591 019 5

Printed and bound in the UK by BPCC Paulton Books Ltd

Bugs Bunny
IN
MUTINY ON THE BUNNY

Story by Norman Redfern

based on an original cartoon

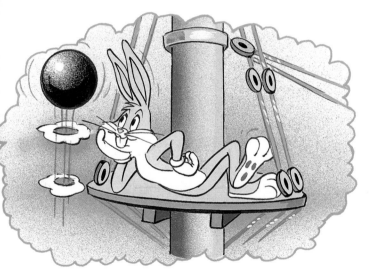

Illustrations by CLIC!

Hi, Bugs Bunny here. I love to travel by sea. The air is so fresh, the waves so relaxing, at the end of the cruise I feel like a new rabbit. I just can't resist stepping off the ship and saying "What's up, dock?"

But not all sea-travel is luxurious. I found that out when I sailed with Shanghai Sam. He tricked me into going aboard the "Sad Sack" with promises of a round-the-world cruise, then sapped me with his cudgel. One minute I was over the moon, the next I was seeing stars.

When I woke up, the ship was at sea, and
so was I. What was I doing with a ball-
and-chain on my ankle? When I asked
the Captain to get rid of it he threw it
overboard. He might have taken it off my
leg first, though.

8

Luckily I'm a strong swimmer. I did the bunny-paddle back to the "Sad Sack", climbed aboard and went to see Shanghai Sam. I was furious with that peppery old salt. I told him there was a little matter we needed to clear up. He handed me the mop!

I was moping at the thought of all that mopping when I had an idea. So he thought he could spring cleaning on me? Well, the pen is mightier than the sud, so I scribbled a few rude messages on the deck. "Look, Captain, Vandals," I cried, and when Sam read the graffiti he snatched the mop and tried to clean up his image.

He'd got the whole deck spotless before he
realised that he'd been tricked. Then he
drew his pistol and told me to furl the
mizzen, or I'd be missin' my fur!

It was time to get my own back on Shanghai Sam. I pretended that the ship had sprung a leak and was in danger of sinking. The sea-fearing Captain believed me and panicked, running around in terror. I've never seen such an ill-bred Admiral flutter by.

The lifeboat was ready, but I wouldn't let the boneless skipper fill it. "The Captain always goes down with his ship," I told him. "Well, I resign," he said.

Sam was desperate to get off the ship
before it sank. He disguised himself as a
little old lady and sat in the lifeboat, ready
to escape.

14

It was time to let him off the hook, for now. Maybe I should have let the lifeboat down a little more gently, but why worry about a drop in the ocean – especially when Sam was doing the dropping!

I wasn't going to let Sam off that lightly.
He was so mean, he even put the ship's cat
out at night. But I had a plan to dampen his
spirits. I dressed the ship's anchor in
rompers and bootees, and called for help
from the dummy in the pram below.
Shanghai Sam was waiting with open arms
to save the "baby", but when I dropped it
from the ship he realised there wouldn't be
a nappy ending.

Captain Sam climbed out of the ocean with seaweed in his hair and revenge on his mind. There was only one thing that would stop him doing something I might regret, and that was his greed for gold. So I told him I had a map that showed where there was buried treasure, and left the detective work to Sam, spade and all.

He followed the directions, paced out the plan and was sure there was gold under that there hull! But when he holed the hold to strike gold, he let in the deep blue sea instead.

The "Sad Sack" sunk, but Shanghai Sam's hopes were still buoyant. He took her back to dry-dock and set about patching her up. The old chiseller was pretty sore, but he knew the drill and couldn't wait to get back to being a crew-driver.

When we set sail again the sun was
shining but Sam was in a stormy mood.
He hadn't forgotten the way I'd tricked him
and was pacing the deck with a loaded
cannon. I was waiting for him in the hold.
When he looked down at me I could see an
enemy!

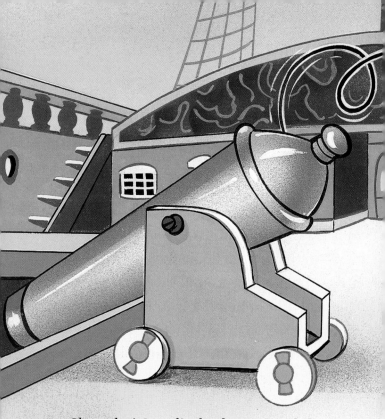

Shanghai Sam lit the fuse, aimed the cannon at me and stood back to wait for the bang. I had a bombshell of my own for him: I wasn't in the hold any more. That's what happens when you don't think things through. But now Sam began to understand what could happen as a result of his hare-trigger, and he desperately tried to put

out the fuse.

It was no use. The cannonball went down to hull and beyond, and the "Sad Sack" went down too.

The "Sad Sack" returned to dry-dock for repairs. She was launched with a fanfare, although half the brass band wasn't there. They were playing in the wrong quay!

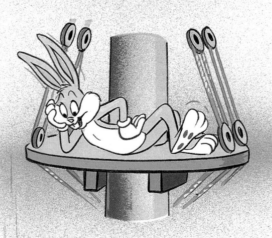

Back on board, Sam was on the rampage again. He spotted my perch in the crow's nest and aimed the cannon at me.

He must have forgotten that there's one law you can't break: the law of gravity. I looked down, and Sam was really having a ball. It's a shame he had to have an early bath!

The ship was moored in dry-dock.
Shanghai Sam had a mean, hungry look
so I let him have an early launch. There
was a dip for starters, then he was in a stew,

and if he ever trifled with me again he'd get
his just desserts. But Shanghai Sam was
beaten at last. Like a Sailor whose hat's a
bit too big, he'd had one capsize too many.

At last! The perfect holiday: sun, sea . . .
and Sam. Still, two out of three's not bad.
Keep rowing, Captain! **,**

Bugs Bunny™